PENGUIN BOOKS

FOR WHOM THE CLOCHE TOLLS

Angus Wilson was born in England in 1913 and was educated at Westminster School and at Oxford University. During the Second World War he worked in the Foreign Office, and since 1963 he has been associated with the University of East Anglia, where he is now Professor of English Literature. His first volume of short stories, *The Wrong Set*, was published when he was thirty-five; this met with immense critical acclaim. His other publications include *Emile Zola* (a short critical study), *The Mulberry Bush* (a play), *A Bit Off the Map* (a collection of short stories), several novels, *Hemlock and After*, *Anglo-Saxon Attitudes*, *The World of Charles Dickens* and *As If By Magic*. Many of his books have been published in Penguins.

Philippe Jullian was born in Bordeaux in 1922 and began to read for a degree in history, but soon preferred drawing and consequently became known in Paris and London as an illustrator of books. He caricatured 'Tout Paris' in the *Dictionaire de snobbisme* and sixteen years ago became a novelist. However his grandfather, Camille Jullian, made him return to history and art criticism. He was a former contributor to *Connaissance des arts* and to the *Revue de Paris*. The translated version of his book *Roberte de Montesquiou* appeared in England in 1967.

FOR WHOM THE CLOCHE TOLLS

A SCRAP-BOOK OF THE TWENTIES

by

Angus Wilson

and

Philippe Jullian

PENGUIN BOOKS

Penguin Books Ltd, Harmondsworth, Middlesex, England
Penguin Books, 625 Madison Avenue, New York, New York 10022, U.S.A.
Penguin Books Australia Ltd, Ringwood, Victoria, Australia
Penguin Books Canada Ltd, 41 Steelcase Road West, Markham, Ontario, Canada
Penguin Books (N.Z.) Ltd, 182–190 Wairau Road, Auckland 10, New Zealand

—

First published 1953
Published by Martin Secker & Warburg 1973
Published in Penguin Books 1976

—

—

Made and printed in Great Britain by
Richard Clay (The Chaucer Press) Ltd,
Bungay, Suffolk
Set in Monotype Perpetua

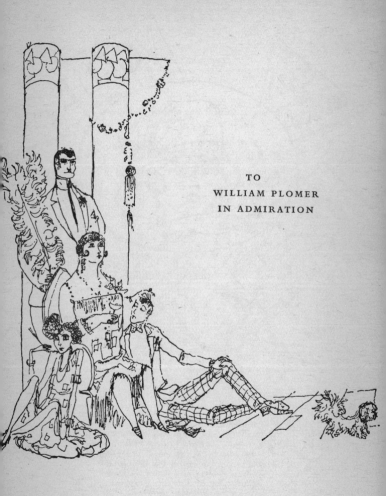

TO
WILLIAM PLOMER
IN ADMIRATION

Busy with my scrap album!
Harold listens in to 2LO and the Savoy Orpheans.

Extract from Alice's Diary

Nov. 12th, 1951.   *St George's Hill,*
Weybridge.

Came back from poor Maisie's funeral tired and depressed, but felt much better after Harold had insisted on mixing me a cocktail. Parsons had been so thoughtful too and prepared just the dinner to cheer me up – a really good fried sole with Sauce Tartare and one of her very best cheese soufflés. Parsons' staying on with us has been the one bright spot of these depressing post-war years. Whenever I think of death – and with poor Maisie's passing on, one inevitably counts the heads that are left; after all, seventy-four is a good age, though I can't say I feel it – I always pray that I shall go before Parsons. It is very selfish of me, I am sure, for what she would do after all these years with us, I *can't* imagine. A day's trip to town is still an event for *her*. But, apart from Harold of course, I really believe that I depend more upon Parsons than *any* one else. I told Parsons about Maisie's funeral, how pitifully few there were there when one remembers all the thousands of people she entertained way back in the twenties, and I even spoke a little of the mass of debts that poor Bridget will have to meet – how Maisie spent all the money living in that horrible little private hotel, I cannot think! – Parsons has been so long with us that she is more a friend of the family than a maid, so that I feel I can talk to her of anything that concerns us. All she said was, 'Poor Mrs Markham! But then she did rather live for herself, didn't she, Madam? It must seem terrible to anyone like you who has always found her pleasure in giving!' I couldn't help feeling happy to be so appreciated, and by one who, after all, knows me so well. I thought it better to say nothing to Parsons about Toby Buller's extraordinary exhibition at the graveside. – So uncontrolled and melodramatic. After all the years he had sponged on poor Maisie, which of course really meant sponging on poor Bridget and me. The whole thing had upset Harold so much that I felt sure he would not wish me to mention it even to so old and loyal a servant.

And now here I am going through my album of snaps and cuttings. It just shows how important and grand Maisie must have seemed to me in those days that I should have taken the trouble to cut out all these pictures of her. I'm afraid *I* figure in very few of them. It was much too smart a world for me, and much too noisy! Even then, I remember, when you could never open the *Tatler* without seeing Maisie's picture, I used sometimes to wonder where it would all end. The very few times that I went to those parties in Eaton Square and later at Hill Street, although of course it was fascinating to meet people who were almost household names and there was a great deal of brilliant talk – my dear friend Sybil Clamber who knew the *really* clever people like Virginia Woolf and Rebecca West always told me that nobody *really* interesting went to Maisie's – but there always seemed to me something 'feverish', I think a writer would call it, about the atmosphere. How cleverly Galsworthy saw and described the brittleness of it all in those later books of his which many people like better than *The Forsyte Saga*, though I think I shall always remain faithful to Old Jolyon.

Of course it was a very *bad* atmosphere for the children to grow up in and, even though Harold didn't really like me going there, I used to go as often as I could just for their sake. I suppose, having no children of my own, I felt more like a mother to them than an aunt. Whatever poor Maisie's virtues, she was *certainly* not cut out to be a mother, as I think my poor brother realized before he died. I remember so well the day that I heard of his death from that terrible Spanish 'flu which carried off so many of one's friends – if we hadn't got so used to those *dreadful* casualty lists it would have seemed even more terrible – my first thought was for Bridget and Tata (we still called him Derek then) and what *would* happen to them with

Maisie a heartbroken widow in 1919 (I wonder!).
The children look sweet.

*Maisie bids farewell to her beloved New York —
so much more her milieu really than England.*

only Maisie to look after them. Of course, they had everything that *money* could buy. Maisie's father was a toothpaste king, though after she got into society she never really liked one to talk of it. Bridget was such a *sweet* young girl, only eighteen! and Tata still a schoolboy and so very earnest! What a time to be deprived of their father's steadying influence! My brother was such a very·*upright* man in carriage *and* in character, as the portrait by Munnings which appears in the photograph shows. And Maisie, poor Maisie, with all her virtues – and let me say it at once she had many – was so very weak and really, I'm afraid, in many ways so dreadfully unsuitable, and what, if she hadn't been my brother's wife, I should have to call vulgar. Of course, it says a great deal for the strength of a really sound strain in a family that, despite everything – and there *were*

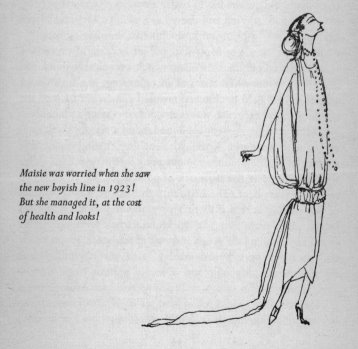

Maisie was worried when she saw
the new boyish line in 1923!
But she managed it, at the cost
of health and looks!

times when it looked as though Tata and even dear Bridget were turning out very badly – in the end, Bridget is such a sweet, good woman and such a wonderful mother to Timothy, and Tata has found a kind of peace – for I suppose living at a Roman Catholic monastery in Chile *is* a kind of peace.

How that funny old photograph recalls it all! We still hadn't got *quite* away from the idea that Woman was a sort of lamp-stand to be hung with decorations. Those great hats and cloaks and veilings! We thought them very pretty, I'm afraid. Of course, we weren't all as excessive as poor Maisie. No matter *how* much she spent on her clothes, she never looked quite right. Her figure didn't really help; it had neither the proportion to be called 'fine' nor the carriage to be called graceful. Later when the more 'petite' figure became fashionable, she tried every ridiculous fad in order to reduce, and, of course, always looked haggard and drawn as a result. But, apart from her figure, she just did not know how to *wear* her clothes. No matter what Paquin or Molyneux did for her, she always added some little colour or ornament which completely destroyed the effect. Even when she was in mourning, she insisted on adding a great gold buckle and tassel! I remember so well the very day this photograph was taken, I was wearing a plain black gabardine coat-frock with appliqué jet and a simple black satin toque with an egret – the whole thing costing about one quarter of Maisie's clothes – and yet I flatter myself . . . But then simplicity is the hallmark of good taste, as we began to see a few years later. The little snap that my nephew Tata took of me pasting scraps into this very album will show what I mean. Just a plain rust silk stockinette frock with jade green jazz design, and a jade green and rust *apache* scarf. It was really the prettiest period imaginable, with its charming neat shingled heads. My hair had a lovely auburn tinge then – Bridget has just the same – and I always wore something green, if only a scarf or handkerchief – to set it off. But I seem to be writing all about myself – Harold would say no woman could

Cecil Beaton's lovely study of Maisie and Bridget, 1929.

resist the temptation to do so! – and I had meant this to be a little tribute to Maisie and the children!

Doesn't dear Bridget look sweet, despite the ugly waistline? I don't think it's just fancy to see already not only the fascinating débutante of Cecil Beaton's famous photograph, but also the splendid wife and mother she is now. There was always something almost royal, I used to think, about her lovely thick gold hair and round surprised china blue eyes – a little prominent, perhaps, but always staring straight ahead. It was never a face very full of expression, laughing and alive like dear old Gladys! nor a 'clever' face like so many of the other girls of her time. Nevertheless, I must say I would give a hundred of the 'clever' girls of those days, now so restless, disappointed and embittered, for the true woman's cleverness which Bridget had shown in managing her home and her children. I have never seen her put herself forward when her husband is speaking – such a clever man, the coming figure on the Conservative back-bench Harold says, but perhaps the tiniest bit pompous – and yet I know, and most of their friends know too, that Bridget can twist him round her finger any day just by a little word or smile. A real British girl! You can see that so clearly in the snap taken at a tennis party I gave for her and Tata in 1921.

Poor Tata! I'm afraid sport was never quite in his line, despite the school blazer he is wearing in the photograph taken just after his father's death. Harold, I'm afraid, never really liked him. He was never a man's man. But, oh dear! he did make me laugh so much! I have only to see the picture I cut out of the *Sketch* which shows dear Aunt Mary talking to Lady Asquith to think of the funny things Tata used to do. He dressed up as Aunt Mary once and gave a talk to the Women's Liberal Association down here at Weybridge. – One would hardly believe it, but I attended the meeting – of course, I have always been Conservative, but the subject 'Women want their Trade Free Too' seemed interesting, and Bridget, naughty

*Aunt Mary and
witty Lady Oxford.*

The awful evening at the Tweedie-Ransomes.

girl! – she knew all along – persuaded me to go – and it was only halfway through when he kept on about Weybridge women being little better than a harem that I realized it was not Aunt Mary at all! Poor old dear, she was so angry when the Liberal party headquarters received complaints. Even then Tata got round her and the next thing we knew she had taken him on an aeroplane trip to Russia to see the Five Year Plan in action. When they came back, she was full of how intelligent he was and how splendidly he had got on with the workers. Of course, he was *very* clever, although he liked to play the 'lounge lizard'. People said he wrote most of Aunt Mary's *A Liberal looks at Lenin's Land* for her, and I shouldn't be a bit surprised if it was true.

I'm afraid Harold never forgave him after the terrible incident at the Tweedie-Ransomes. In Harold's opinion the Tweedie-Ransomes used to be the most important people in England. I always thought them a bit stuffy and pleased with themselves. But Sir Alfred was a very brilliant eye surgeon and Harold, being a doctor, naturally sees people from rather a medical point of view. Tata met them down here at one of my garden fêtes when he kindly took on the palmist's booth for me, and Lady Tweedie-Ransome was so excited by the fortune he foretold for her that they became firm friends. What was my horror when their daughter Ada rang me up one day in a terrible state to say that both Sir Alfred and his wife were in a nursing home with nervous prostration. It was quite a new thing then and I made Harold so annoyed when I told him that Sir Alfred had been taken ill with prostate. I'm afraid I'm very inclined to make terrible gaffes! What had happened apparently was that the wretched T-R.s were sitting in their rather over-furnished drawing-room in Devonshire Place when suddenly a whole fleet of cars drew up and out rushed Tata and a crowd of his bright young friends. Lady T-R. never spoke to me again, but I heard from another friend that she described what followed as worse than the Armenian Massacre. Apart from wrecking their room, Tata's friends poured a whole bottle of gin down Lady T-R.'s throat, while Bridget and that extraordinary friend of hers Eupenthe Bristowe climbed all over Sir Alfred's knee. Of course, he adored it really – even Harold had to admit that no pretty girl who was the faintest bit shortsighted (and so many of them, of course, were) was safe in his consulting-room – but he had to pretend to be furious because of Lady T-R., and *she* was livid because she thought that the joke with the gin was a reference to the notorious fact that she was a secret drinker! They made a terrible fuss about their old drawing-room, though I'm sure there was nothing that a dustpan and brush couldn't have put right in half an hour. Tata, as usual, got round the old lady by taking cartloads of roses to the nursing home and when the matron came in, she was out of bed learning to Charleston! I was the one who suffered really, because Harold didn't get invited to the T-R.'s next *soirée*, but Tata took me out to a wonderful lunch at the Basque where we sat next to beautiful Lady Diana and her clever mother. I wanted to go to a matinée of Marie Tempest, but Tata persuaded me into a beauty salon. I was terrified of what Harold would say about the expense, but Tata just put it down to Maisie's account and I must say that, when she saw me afterwards, she had the grace to admit that it had been well worth the money.

I don't want to give the idea that Bridget and Tata were just butterflies, though, with their mother's example before them, that would not have been surprising. But, not at all. Tata had the most wonderful capacity for getting on with all *kinds* and *classes* of people. He really should have been a writer. He was quite splendid during the General Strike, and volunteered as a tram conductor. Poor boy! he was set on by a crowd of terrible men who said they were picketing or some such nonsense, and, although he received a dreadful black eye, he only said that he was quite ready to go through it all again. One of the men came to see him afterwards to say how sorry he was

Tata made me go to a beauty salon,
as you will read in my diary.

and he and Tata became firm friends. For a time too, Tata insisted on earning his own living! He played the piano at a little cinema near King's Cross Station, a terrible, dark little place. It became quite fashionable to go there and he used to play different tunes for all his friends – I remember going one afternoon and just because he knew I was there, he played my favourite *Kitten on the Keys* ten times for me. In the end the management said he was distracting the audience from the screen, so he gave the job up and made lampshades at home for friends. Both he and Bridget were always clever with their fingers – poor Maisie could hardly do up a shoe-button! – and as I was very busy in those days making necklaces out of scraps of wallpaper, we used to have many a sewing bee together! Bridget used to make the most lovely batik scarves that were quite professional. The little snapshot shows her before she had her hair cut, with two lovely coils over her ears. It looked just like cloth of gold! Harold, who was always very fond of his niece, used to make fun of her ear-phones – 'Listening in to the Savoy Orpheans?' he used to ask. Later on, about 1927, when they were both a little older and found being at home with Maisie rather a strain I think, they started a hat shop with a little cocktail bar attached. Tata had a real *flair* for millinery and of course waiting husbands or cavaliers were always more ready to foot the bill after Bridget's clever cocktails. Dear old Gladys – you can see her snap opposite to Bridget's, when she

Tata was never just a lounge-lizard.
The rich, after all, were not so idle.

pluckily took on work as a mannequin to pay off her father's gambling debts – always said that if they'd only had a business sense, the hat shop would have been a gold mine. In any case, they were only running it for fun, of course.

We sometimes used to think that fun was all they thought about with their surprise parties and treasure hunts, but I always knew that if the need came, they would turn up trumps. Poor children! Yes, I doubt if anyone who just looked through this scrap album with its continuous round of parties and pleasure could guess just how strained things were in that ménage. I'm always so happy to think how both Tata and Bridget confided in me and came to me to 'get it off their chests'. I sometimes think that my brother's death must have affected poor Maisie's head a little. Of course, she had never been *completely* faithful to him, but I'm glad to say I have never been a prude, and as I used to say to Harold 'The world of Claridges and Deauville is not St George's Hill.' She was, as a young bride, both a lovely and a silly girl, but although she was 'liée' more than once after her marriage, it was always with men of her own standing, 'hommes du monde' like Colonel Croxe-Filly. She was never, I'm afraid, as discreet as she should have been. I was horrified to learn only recently from Bridget how much both she and Tata knew of their mother's amours even *before* my poor brother's death. But still there was nothing *really* unpleasant, but afterwards . . . well, I dare say one could find a lot of 'psychological' names to make it sound better, but the plain truth is that she was *man mad*. If it hadn't been for the children, of course, it would just have been *pathetic*, but, as it was, I find it *very* difficult to excuse her. A woman of forty (and Maisie was thirty-nine when dear Roger died) who runs after any and everything in trousers is ridiculous enough, but a mother of two children at the impressionable age! Had she been forty-five, even, one might have found a hundred little excuses, Nature plays such strange tricks with us. But as it was! I suppose when one thinks of

Bridget and Tata were full of pluck and clever ideas, as this combined modiste-cocktail bar (1926) shows.

some of the tragedies that infatuation with younger men brought in those days – those stupid, passionate letters of that poor feather-brained Edith Thompson, and later Mrs Rattenbury (I remember how upset I was to think how easily *she* might have been one's own neighbour – shopping at Harrods and staying at quite a smart residential hotel with her own *chauffeur*). And of course Mrs Barney, who was quite a friend

of Maisie's. (Such different backgrounds, and yet not one of them disreputable. I'm afraid the horror of the First World War affected us all a great deal more deeply than we realized.) When, indeed, I think of *some* of Maisie's 'friends', I'm amazed that things did not turn out worse than they did. That '*affaire*' with the boxer – one writes '*affaire*' but really these little French words which seem so appropriate to the indiscretions

Edith Thompson (a tragic figure!) Frederick Bywaters (so young and yet so strange a hold over her!) What cannot love do to human beings!

of people of one's own class hardly fit anything so sordid – which caused such a scandal at the time, took place, thank God! in America, but even so the rumours over here were painful enough. Harold was so upset that he almost forbade me to go to Eaton Square, but I was determined to do what I could for my own brother's children. I shall never forget, too, the day that Bridget appeared here suddenly in her little sports car. It was a lovely autumn day, of 1926, and as she stepped out of her little 'bus', I remember thinking how beautiful she seemed against the yellowing chestnut leaves in her little lemon frock with its sash patterned in leaves of stencilled coppery velvet. Her trim little figure seemed almost waif-like in the short low-waisted frock which we should now think so ugly and her funny little *retroussé* nose and round blue eyes looked out from under her cloche and seemed to say 'Where am I, please? I'm lost.' And so for the moment, poor darling, she was. It was lucky that Harold was out that morning, for she was near to tears, and he detests any kind of scene. I would not allow her to talk to me of her troubles until we had lunched – Parsons turned up trumps once again with Cutlets Reform and one of her best crème caramel. And then as we sat over our little coffee cups, she told me: It was such a sad little young girl's worry – a little love affair that had gone awry – and yet again it wasn't – for the other woman was her own mother! Even now I can remember that it left a nasty little taste in the mouth – more bitter than the black coffee we had been drinking. Poor child, like all the rest of her generation, she was dance mad and like many others she had fallen very much in love with . . . a gigolo. I don't think there would have been very much harm in it. Some people would say 'A dancing professional! A man who took money to partner rich women for the evening!' but then the same people would probably say 'A Brazilian!' I would be more inclined to think poor silly old women who imagine that because a penniless young foreigner teaches them to dance and flirts a little with them, he is in love with them.

The awful depths to which Maisie's 'man madness' led her.
Brooklyn 1925.

But he *was* in love with Bridget, I think, a little; they were both young, they both loved dancing. It would hardly have meant much, just a pretty pirouette like the falling chestnut leaves – they would have danced and kissed and sworn eternal love . . . and parted. And neither would have been very hurt. W. J. Locke might have written of it, a little sentimentally, or Michael Arlen with a touch of cynicism. But what poor Bridget could not have expected, what even Somerset Maugham would not have imagined, was Maisie. A mother of forty-five who just walks in and flashes her jewels and her cheque book and, after she has captured the weak, silly boy, flaunts the more sordid aspects in her daughter's face. I tried hard to believe that Bridget had misunderstood, but it was no good. I can see her now, her little hand clenching her handkerchief in anger, her blue eyes almost hard. 'No, Alice dear,' she said. 'You don't quite understand Maisie yet. She's a bitch and she'll stop at nothing!' Poor child! her little Cartier diamond bracelet flashed in the sunlight as she released the brake of her car and, as she sped away, I thought, 'Clever Noel Coward! Poor little rich girl indeed!'

It really looked to me then as though Bridget might walk out of her mother's life for ever. Perhaps in some ways it would have been best, but a mother – even one like Maisie – is an important thing in a young girl's life. So I did all I could to repair the breach. I invited all three of them out to gay little evenings, gay but without the feverish search for gaiety of their usual round. It would give them, I thought, a chance to let the bitter cross-currents fade away in simple pleasure, would rest their jangled nerves. I remember so well an evening when I tried to divert them by teaching them Mah-Jong. Bridget, poor dear! seemed *distraite* and almost haggard. She had already had too many cocktails when she arrived and she was quarrelsome with Maisie, trying to assert her freedom by using bad language. Tata, I must confess, was frankly bored. Strangely enough, only Maisie seemed really to enter into the

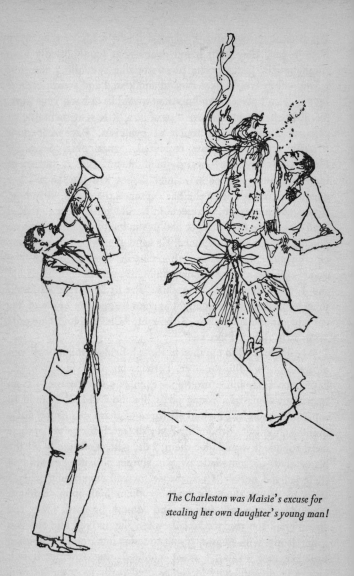

The Charleston was Maisie's excuse for stealing her own daughter's young man!

game. She was always a passionate gambler and, although the stakes had to be low to suit my modest income, she was soon absorbed in her love of winning. As I looked at her that evening, her ample figure almost bursting from her black *charmeuse* evening dress, her jade-holder held tightly in her spoilt little mouth, I thought 'If only you could be your age you might be quite a pleasant, happy woman!'

But then, of course, if she had been her age, she would not have been Maisie! Tata used to tease me about it, I remember, 'Poor old Maisie, if she can manage to look thirty-five, Alice darling, at least it's amusing. As for the rest, she's just "naturally loving" darling, like *Nigger Heaven*. Don't be a Dora, dear. It's you and Mr Joynson-Hicks, that's what it is!' But I remember well how differently he felt when she began running after a young friend of his. Of course, he was right, in a way, with these boxers and gigolos she was only harming herself, but when it came to a nice boy like Dick Mutton who had such a fine career ahead of him in the Navy, that was very different. Poor Lady Mutton was so upset, she was most anxious for him to marry that nice girl of the Hetherstoke-Puleys. How Maisie did it nobody knew! She was forty-seven by then and Dick was twenty-five. Tata's distress for his friend was really quite touching. 'It isn't as if I minded about her having fun, Alice darling,' he said to me, 'but Dickie's so different, hardly at all "bloody male". And after all, she's forty-five, dear. No, I'm sorry, but *ça me repugne un peu.*' Tata always spoke a language of his own, but he was a sincere friend to Dick Mutton; even the silver cord by which Maisie tried to hold her son couldn't stand up to what he felt was wrong where his friends were concerned.

Only once did I have it out with Maisie herself, and then she was so strange, almost childish. 'It's easier for you, Alice,' she said; 'you don't get blue and bore everyone to hell. But *I* do unless I take any fun that comes my way, and then, you know, other people *do* get a *bit* of the fun as well, so it's quite good

My little attempt to give them all simpler pleasures in life.
A Mah-Jong party 1926.

all round.' Well, I mean, really! Such irresponsibility is not quite sane.

A Sensible Note of Harold's about Maisie

I cannot say that I feel entirely happy about my dear wife's idea of circulating, even privately, a memoir of my late sister-in-law. Our great-nephew Timothy has shown considerable enthusiasm over the scheme. His grandmother, he tells us, was the embodiment of her age – what, I understand, the popular Press refers to as the 'Naughty Twenties'. It is strange how the illusion persists that those who make the most noise are the most important. In the years immediately after that curious mixture of pig-headed selfishness and utopian bungling that Lloyd George and President Wilson concocted at Versailles, there was, of course, a good deal of irresponsible clowning and the youth of the day sowed a little more than its fair share of wild oats. People had been through a bad time and it was only natural that they should want to let off steam a bit. The older and more level-headed of us stood back and waited until the mafficking was over. We didn't have long to wait either. In a couple of years, the nation as a whole had settled down to its normal everyday jog-trot. People had work to attend to and they got on with it. The coalition – always an unhealthy thing in peace time – was brought to an end and under Baldwin – a much maligned man who knew his job – that remarkable animal the British public set about doing what it always likes best – minding its own business. Of course there were a lot of old women of both sexes, of whom Alice's Aunt Mary was typical, who gassed away about the League of Nations – but nobody in this country took much notice of them; we're used to our professional bazaar-openers, and if there aren't any bazaars for them to open at home, they have to get themselves

Aunt Mary flew to Leningrad in 1926. She was so very hopeful on her return. The worst excesses of the Revolution seemed over. But Harold, who was really much wiser though not a politician, was always suspicious of a thing like the Five Year Plan.

mixed up in grandiose schemes abroad. There was a tiny fraction too, of course, who went on behaving as though the whole of life was one long Armistice celebration. People with too much money, too little sense and no tradition. My sister-in-law Maisie was one of these.

They let themselves go in an orgy of parties and divorces and thought themselves very clever because they'd found out how to break the Seventh Commandment. I remember I once asked my sister-in-law if she thought adultery was a new discovery. These things, I told her, were as old as time and as long as people kept quiet about them, it was entirely their own affair. But when a lot of nobodies find that every foolish thing they do gets reported in the papers, there's no holding them; and so it was with the much advertised 'Bright Young Things', to whom Maisie, who was quite old enough to have known better, belonged. She had some excuse, of course, because she came from some God-forsaken town in the Middle West. I'm the last person who would wish to say anything against the Americans in these days, but they *are* different from us and any attempt to pretend otherwise is very foolish. In any case, my sister-in-law was never an honest-to-God American whom I would be the first to respect, but an expatriate, one of the international idle rich, as the soap-box orators like to call them. That indeed was the trouble with the whole of Maisie's set – they were without roots. Unfortunately they had enough money to make a spectacle of themselves and there were those who were only too pleased to let them do so. In my humble opinion, it is no small degree the result of their irresponsibility and bad breeding for which we are paying today in general slackness and mistrust of leadership. With all due respect to Kipling, who had more blind spots than is generally realized, 'the Colonel's lady and Judy O'Grady' may be all very true, but it misses the real point. When Maisie and her friends gave a very good public imitation of the morals of washerwomen, every washerwoman in the country – I use the term figuratively,

Aunt Mary was tireless in her work for the poor! Here she is outside her husband's factory speaking to his former employees on the work of the League of Nations Union and the I.L.O.

Freud and sex were all the thing then! Aunt Mary, who took an intelligent interest in everything, was one of the first to consult a psychoanalyst in 1922. She resented the analysis of her political interests I'm afraid!

of course, and intend no disrespect to what I have no doubt is a very decent and hardworking section of the community – loved to read about it in the Sunday papers, but bang went every inch of respect that she had for her betters, and who could blame her? I have no desire to speak ill of the dead – 'de mortuis' is in general the golden rule – but if this memoir is to be published, I can only hope that it will serve to illustrate how empty and uninteresting were the lives of that very unrepresentative and vocal minority whom it is apparently now the fashion among the Bright Young Things of our own day to admire.

It is, indeed, only for this reason that I have consented to add my note to those of the rest of the family; and I have purposely chosen a little anecdote about my late sister-in-law that may illustrate what I mean. It was in the summer of 1927 that she came to ask my advice on a personal and financial matter. I suppose I should have been flattered by this unexpected attention. Maisie was certainly not without men to advise her, but for all her foolishness, she was not without certain moments of level-headed shrewdness, inherited no doubt from her business forebears. She was happy to flirt or more with the wastrels she had collected around her, but when it came to money matters she looked to more solid advice. I flatter myself that she could not have chosen more wisely. Every professional man needs a hobby and mine has always been the interplay of the market. Apart from its intrinsic interest, there is no truer touchstone of a man's worth than his reaction to the rise and fall of his shares; but to be successful in the field you need that cool and steady judgement of men and women which, though the man in the street little realizes it, is the *sine qua non* of every successful G.P.'s career.

The problem that Maisie brought to me needed, I saw at once, both careful financial consideration and a balanced judgement of humanity's failings. Her story was a simple one: She wanted to pension off one of her lovers and, as he was

43

A more healthy side of English life than the Bright Young People! Harold's nephews and nieces — the Bunglebys — adored hiking. They only met Bridget and Tata once, but I'm afraid it wasn't a success. Elspeth Bungle used to attend ALL *the Nuremberg rallies in the 1930s, but that was when we only knew the* GOOD *side of Hitler!*

many years younger than herself, she had a bad conscience and was anxious to make sure that the pension would be so tied up that it would give him future security and allow her to bury her misgivings in the belief that she had planned for his future. It was not a pretty picture and my first inclination was to wash my hands of the matter entirely. There is an ugly word for men who are willing to live on women and any man of decency

44

will apply it immediately. I did so and in no uncertain terms. But, as I have already said, my professional experience has not allowed me to wear rose-coloured spectacles. It would be pleasant to judge men and women by the ordinary standards of decency but it would be foolish. The situation had to be viewed as it was, not as it would appear in story books – except as it would have been seen in those cynical perhaps, but

DAMES

*Russian nobility showed pluck
everywhere in adapting themselves
to strange jobs.*

eminently real pictures of humanity that our greatest writer Somerset Maugham has given us. I began by administering a cold douche to her sentimentality. I would see the fellow, I said, and arrange a settlement with him on business terms, as favourable and economic terms to herself as possible, but I would do so on commission. The matter was a business one and must be treated as such; the sooner she realized that the better. Her immediate response, of course, was an incoherent outpouring of romantic nonsense. She was still in love with him, had no wish to end the *affaire*, had simply wished to make provision for his future without his knowing it. I took it upon

Eupenthe Bristowe

Silly America! As if you can save your orchard by putting up a notice 'Little boys are forbidden to steal apples'. Prohibition, as any Englishman could have told them, was disastrous — Gangsters, young people blinded and heaven knows what horrors!

myself to disregard this without informing her – for her own interest.

The fellow turned out to be a professional dancing partner, a South American. I afterwards learnt from Alice that his first designs had been upon my niece Bridget but that when he had realized there was nothing doing in that quarter, he had transferred his attentions to the mother! ! He turned out to be much as I expected: a professional adventurer with the sort of flashy good looks which are so often the ruin of women of my late sister-in-law's stamp. At first, of course, he met my suggestions for a sensible arrangement with an exhibition fitted for grand opera – he loved Maisie, he was not to be insulted, in fact nobody was to be insulted but myself; however, I let him go on and simply reiterated the plain business facts of the situation. My sister-in-law was a woman of very generous heart, I pointed out, who felt a duty where quite frankly none existed. I was there, of course, to protect her interests and so on. As I expected, I had almost closed the door behind me, when the fellow changed his tune . . . if everything was over, well, then, he had his family to consider, his mother, he assured me, was very old. It was all very sordid and very much as the world goes. The long and the short of it was that I secured Maisie from his further attentions at a much lower rate than her own hare-brained nature would have succeeded in doing – and he, if I know the Latin races, intended to establish some little restaurant or other that would give him a nice *rente* to raise a family on.

Unfortunately, I had estimated Maisie's stupidity insufficiently. A storm broke over my head. Of course, she said, she had known that the *affaire* would eventually come to an end, but this early and sensible conclusion, it seemed, was not what she wanted. There must be tears and scenes and reconciliations and protestations of love all round to satisfy her. It had not, I suggested, required so much expense of emotion to satisfy him. And then the full extent of her stupidity was revealed – she was perfectly aware, she said, that Luis – that was the fellow's name – had a mercenary side, could, in fact, be bought, but so had we all and it was monstrous and wrong apparently to expose such things. She had no wish to make him expose himself; her happiness came, she told me, from giving him everything that kept him sweet and romantic, and now I had shattered that happiness. Anybody could break illusions, she told me, the point of existence was to preserve them. Of course, after that, I washed my hands of the whole affair;

indeed, if I had not felt that it would have been wrong, I would have indulged my own pride by returning the commission.

I heard later that after a few months of throwing lavish presents at him, the thing ended by Maisie buying him a restaurant at three times the cost I had estimated and fitting it up herself. When Alice remonstrated with her, she simply replied that she liked furnishing restaurants and that, if Luis had been left to do it himself, being Latin he would have ruined everything by cheeseparing over details.

Josephine Baker. Such an extravagant figure with her leopards!

Parties! Parties! They were the essence of Maisie's life. The 'Tatler' noticed them, the 'Daily Express' complained of them, but the rest of England went on with the real process of living.

A sweet letter from dear Bridget

Grassthorpe Manor,
Huntingdonshire.

Darling Alice,

I did think it was awfully sweet of you and Uncle Harold to come to that dreadful funeral; both Roger and I appreciated it very much. We didn't tell you at the time but poor Mummy had left a special letter saying that she wanted to be cremated!! She said funerals seemed to her such depressing ceremonies. Poor darling! it was terribly like her in a way, as though one could avoid the sad things that happen by just wishing that they wouldn't. And as if, in any case, a cremation with all that awful solemn ugliness – do you remember Aunt Mary's? – wasn't far more depressing. Roger and I debated and debated, because after all if somebody does express a wish, one has to consider it carefully, however irresponsible, but I felt that if Tata heard that Mummy had been cremated he'd never forgive me – you know how Catholics are! – so we compromised on that rather sad little London ceremony. I would have dearly loved to have held it in the village church here, and I know that Roger felt that too – after all the village church must be the real centre of English life, if, that is, England is ever to be something again, but Timothy made a terrible fuss about it – aren't the young strange? – and as he felt Mummy's death so dreadfully we felt we *had* to compromise. He went on a lot about Mummy's basic integrity – poor darling, she had a lot of virtues but integrity! I almost told him about all the debts Roger has paid in these last years, but I don't think one should shatter idols in a moment of emotion – he seems to have regarded Mummy as the embodiment of the nineteen-twenties – though what on earth the child can know about that pre-historic period I can't imagine – and with his set at Oxford the 'twenties are a sort of golden age. Roger says it's quite under-

Our supposed idle rich! Gladys (a fine old family hers) was a superb model!
Bridget made batik scarves!

standable when one thinks of the dreary austerity of University life now compared with when he was up, and, of course, we *did* have fun and the 'twenties were better than the hysteria and wish fulfilment of the years that followed. But poor Mummy could hardly have been called the *embodiment* of any age. I don't think she was really ever quite conscious of what year was what or of having grown up at all. I expect the London funeral was all for the best, really, because Mummy always hated the country, and, even after all the years she had

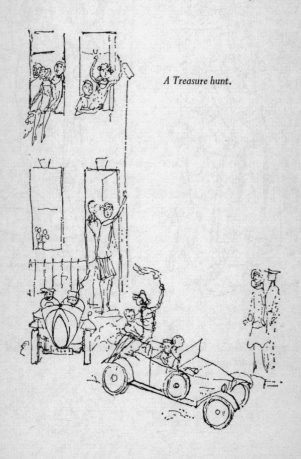

A Treasure hunt.

lived here, she was never *really* English. We had no *idea*, of course, that that dreadful Toby Buller was going to appear and weep whisky tears – I'm afraid poor Uncle Harold was terribly upset – but, as he *was* there I thought we had better make the best of it and be as polite as possible. Thank God we need never see him again! I think he had some extraordinary idea that Mummy would leave what little she had to him, though how he dared to suppose she had anything to leave after the way he had *battened* all these years passes understanding. Actually I was awfully pleased that she *did* leave everything to

Timothy, because I never quite knew how much she appreciated the hours he spent with her – practically the whole of last summer vacation when we expected him up here. Where any *man* was concerned she *did* rather tend to take every attention for granted. I suppose, in a way, that was what they liked.

I'm not going to pretend that I've been shattered or anything, because I haven't. We were never terribly close – *you* know what our childhood was like – and since I was married (for which, dear Aunt, I have to thank you) we've had less and less in common. All the same the past *is* there and it has naturally come back a lot in these last few days.

Poor Mummy! I suppose I ought to say 'poor Maisie', for one of the earliest lessons she drummed into us was that we should call her by her Christian name. Tata, of course, would have done so anyway, I don't think he could speak to anyone without using their Christian names, except for strangers and then he always called them 'darling'. I always hated it, though. Every now and again I used to revolt and say 'Mother'. I did it one day, I remember, at a dress show. Mummy was in a stinking temper already, because we'd just seen a lot of new designs for the 'boyish line' and at that time she was still very much in possession of a bust and hips. She achieved miracles of course, in the weeks that followed, but slim and young even in a way though she did get to look, I always hated it. There's something rather horrid about having one's Mother taken for oneself at a distance, and then, too, it made the poor darling more than ever jealous of me. While she could still keep a woman's figure I don't think she minded having me about half so much; after all, *she* had a fine figure and I was just skimpy and immature, but once the boyish line came in there was bound to be rivalry, and she, poor dear, could only *hope* to compete with the half-light and distance on her side. Aren't I being catty? I suppose it's years of suppressed feelings, and then Timothy saying all those silly things about her integrity the other day made me boil over.

The terrible South American family of whom Bridget writes!

What I suppose I really hated from the beginning was that she *never* made us respect her, never even wanted to. She and Tata were a bit alike there – although, of course, Tata was so much cleverer – as long as everything went smoothly and was cosy they didn't care what happened. She had no *standards*, Alice darling, and I think even from quite a little girl I wanted somebody to look up to when Daddy was away, because of course he was my *hero*. I think, perhaps, that was why I loved Nanny so much; she was comic of course and not a tiny bit elegant – and even then I liked things to look nice – but she *did* make a difference between what was right and what was wrong and we knew that it would be the *same* difference every day, like having the same cakes every day and going the same walks (Tata always wanted something different). But Mummy always behaved *exactly* as she felt, and she always seemed to feel such a lot about everything. She couldn't meet someone at a party or see a new hat without 'loving' it or 'hating' it. I think that was why I liked coming down to Weybridge (although you and Uncle Harold could be so stuffy and dis-approving about all sorts of things that were tremendous fun, like that Treasure Hunt where Eupenthe filled Mrs Moles-worth's lavatory with baby turtles) because you and Uncle only felt strongly about things that weren't talked about. I suppose it was very difficult for Mummy being American – and, of course, the kind of American she was. Did you ever see Granny Ponder? Tata and I used to call her Cook of Cook's Tours, she was just like a jolly barmaid on a holiday – but it *did* make it difficult for us. We could never go anywhere without her making an entrance – always the wrong sort – and then she was always either being over-lavish with tips or making scenes. She had a terrible habit too, of picking up *just* the wrong sort of people. There's a photo somewhere – I believe you've got it – of a dreadful South American family she wished on Tata and me at the Crillon one Easter. Of course, in the end Tata got very gay with the mother – you know what he was about

Bridget's little idyll in Paris!

Aunt Mary presents Bridget at court.
Bridget looked like a fairy-tale princess!

overdressed middle-aged women – and then Mummy became jealous and had a terrible row at La Rues. For once I remember I lost my temper and wandered about Paris all the afternoon on my own until quite the sweetest but most unsuitable little Frenchman tried to pick me up. It was quite horrid, I remember, having to snub him, but I let him have my address so that he could send me a snap he had taken of me looking most innocent and *jeune anglaise*. The poor silly creature bombarded me with passionate love letters for ages afterwards. Of course,

I never answered them, but I sometimes tease Roger about it when he is being difficult.

Yes, darling, you were more of an anchor than perhaps you realized in those days. You and, of course, Aunt Mary. Darling Aunt Mary! so kind-hearted and so full of everything boring in life – the League of Nations and visiting Russia and not visiting Mussolini and always on and on about the age of youth and youth's big chance and then hating everything young people ever wanted to do. I was only thinking at Mummy's funeral when Roger was blaming Mr Baldwin and regretting how irresponsible we had all been in those days not having given the country a lead, that he just hadn't known Aunt Mary. Poor sweet, she never stopped giving the country a lead, at bazaars and conferences and country houses, and at dinners in funny hotels like the Hotel Metropole, but the lead she gave was so boring that even her own relations couldn't listen to it let alone the country. And, after all, Aunt Mary *was* politics in the 'twenties, pioneering in aeroplane flights and talks from Savoy Hill, saying things to Litvinoff and being awfully good with Mrs Snowden. I can't think of a more depressing life, and though I see that we *were* awfully irresponsible and laid the way for the dreadful, earnest progressive young men that I used to see at her house just before she died (you know, when her kindness of heart led her into that silly Spanish business) I still think it was very understandable. All the same she was kind, and I thank God for her every time I see that picture of myself in that terrible dress I was presented at Court in. The shape of the skirt! and the lace at the bottom that looked like fringing! and poor Aunt Mary's single ostrich plume! She was a bit worried about feathers because her dear friend Jennie Hampshire was busy agitating against the cruelty of wearing them, but I remember she assured me that ostriches just *dropped* their feathers, as well they might considering how hideous they were. You probably never knew that there was an awful moment when Mummy threatened to present me. Of course, she couldn't and she was furious. Wouldn't it have been awful? Or rather, it would either have been a wonderful evening or the most shaming experience of one's life. But with Aunt Mary it was dull and correct and that was what I always wanted.

Of course, Mummy could be enchanting and do the most understanding things, usually when Tata had explained to her what we wanted. She put us into that mews flat in 1926 you know, when Tata did all that professional dancing that wasn't very good. *And* she didn't come to the party we gave when

Bridget and Tata give a party in their mews flat.

Eupenthe fell over the balcony, which was very understanding of her.

Sometimes I think she would have loved to have been the conventional mother, but she just didn't know the way to do it. You know how we look in the Beaton photograph; of course, she was getting a bit tired by then and as a result we got on much better, but all the same she was quite sweet and understanding that day and I think you can see it in the photograph.

Everything, in fact, was all right with Mummy so long as

We REALLY knew what overcrowding meant in those days!

nothing went wrong, which isn't quite good enough, is it? That, of course, was what made her show up so badly when the crash came. That awful Match King! Roger laughs at me because I still have a thing about matches. Everything would probably have disappeared in the Wall Street crash anyway, Mummy could never stop speculating. She had terribly little sense of property, as Roger says, 'You can't breed tradition in one generation.' But the Kreuger thing was very dramatic. We were at Juan-les-Pins when Gladys read it out of the paper. She was terribly upset because Mummy had persuaded her to

Bridget, looking so lovely in her beach pyjamas and beach hat, looks calmly on while Maisie makes a show of herself on learning that they have 'crashed' in 1930. Gladys looks a real 'guy' reading out the news! The young man on the ground was a brilliant young friend of Tata's who later went in for Yogi!

put the bit of money her father had left her into the same business. Actually it was almost nothing, though you would have thought from the fuss she made that she'd lost millions. She kept on saying it was her all, but really, when an all is as small as that, it's silly to call it an all, don't you think? However, Mummy was far too busy having hysterics to take notice of anyone else's losses. It was just the kind of melodrama she enjoyed. I'm afraid I was quite unable to help her. I just wanted to be left alone, not to be where people could sympathize and be inquisitive, to have time to think and lay plans for the

future, to find some way of avoiding the sort of shabby gentility which I knew at once would be Mummy's easy way out. Tata was in Retreat at the time, so that I had only myself to rely on in order to escape being mixed up in Mummy's hysteria and easy tears.

She was frightened, Alice, that was what disgusted me so much. The next few days were pandemonium. At one minute we were utterly ruined and she preferred suicide! The next, everything would be all right really and she was dancing with that French boy Raoul as though nothing had happened! At the back of her mind, of course, she just thought *I* would cope and that would be that. I shall never forget her state when I told her that I had wired to Aunt Mary and that I proposed to stay at Portman Square. She stormed and threatened and implored me to stay. It wasn't altogether easy but I knew that I must stand outside if I was to survive, and I knew, in a way too, that she would fall on her feet. Water in the face is an old remedy for hysteria, Nanny used to say, but it's the best one. How right she was!

Living at Aunt Mary's was rather a strain, but then Roger came on the scene, and thanks to you, darling, and your advice everything turned out as I could never have dreamed. Did you ever know that Mummy wrote me the most extraordinary letter when she read of my engagement? We hadn't written to each other all that year. She was living in some *pension* in Cannes, but she didn't seem to mind. Her letter was all about some system she'd found for playing *chemin-de-fer* and how she was growing her hair and that she'd really decided she

No reporters! Such is fame! Bridget the most photographed young débutante of 1925 is now just any bride of 1931. They had lost their money. Roger (how sound and able he looks) is not yet an M.P. Maisie, who had cared not a halfpenny for Bridget's welfare, has to act the tragic mother, of course. My Brownie wouldn't work, so that this picture taken by Roger's sister Heather was **a godsend!**

liked American men best anyway. It was only in the last paragraph that she referred to Roger at all and that was only to say that she'd always hoped for something better for me, but that perhaps I didn't mind English middle-class life as much as she did! She ended by telling me that she would try to come to the wedding if she got an invitation to stay with Mai Ricochet, but that we must'nt expect her to come up to Huntingdonshire because she hated fields and dogs.

Well, apparently Mai did ask her to stay, because as you know she came to the wedding and wept. I was rather glad really because I would have hated any sort of unconventional absence, and so would Roger.

We used to get letters and postcards from all over Europe in the 'thirties, but it wasn't until the War that I saw her again. She seemed so washed up and pitiful, but as soon as Uncle Harold and Roger had put her money affairs in order she was quite happy again. I always tried to avoid talking about money to her, because one felt so unhappy about her being dependent. But I really don't believe she cared at all as long as it was there. Staying in those ghastly hotels and playing bridge all day! For some reason or other, she wouldn't leave London even during the worst of the raids. It made Roger so angry; as he said, nobody who was not doing useful work should have got in the way of the authorities. But after she met that terrible Toby Buller, no one could move her. You'll be shocked at what I'm going to say, darling, and it does seem a little odd about one's own mother, but I'm afraid she had the temperament of a tart, she was perfectly happy so long as she had a man.

Tata's clever letter

Alice's note: After Bridget's sweet remarks, I am afraid that Tata's answer to my letter will seem very strange. I can only say that he was a dear, lovable boy, but, of course, always very

London went crazy over the Black Birds. Dear
generous-hearted Florence Mills! Her early death
was as tragic in its way as Meggie Albanesi's.

clever. If he seems to speak of their childhood as less unhappy than dear Bridget, it was always, of course, easier for a boy. Maisie spoilt him and men all like that. Then again, although I always believe that everyone should have his or her *own* religion (each one of them surely has something of the Truth in it) there is no doubt that Roman Catholics have a very strange *moral* sense. As Harold said the other day they've learnt for so long to chop words about that one sometimes fears they've almost forgotten the difference between right and wrong. Nobody can deny, however, that Tata's is a very *clever* letter, especially for these days when the art of letter writing seems almost to have disappeared.

Dear Aunt Alice,

As you so truly said in your letter to me, Maisie's death 'was bound to occur sooner or later'. Such 'inevitabilities' are not surely ever very far from our thoughts, unless fear of life has completely numbed our sense of its meaning. Maisie's death, you write, was 'in many ways a happy release'. I have pondered a lot on that 'in many ways', dear Aunt Alice. In any final sense, I cannot, of course, imagine how death could be anything but 'happy' release – surely something so far beyond words that 'happy' must seem odd – for all but so few – and none of us may judge who those few may be – certainly, for Maisie, wayward, lost though she was, a happiness beyond any words. But if you mean that she, like so many lost souls today, was 'glad to go', as they still say I believe (I live so far away that for all I know the whole English vocabulary may have changed overnight), then I cannot agree with you. With all her faults and follies, Maisie had a 'natural' understanding of life's joys which I have only seen equalled (*and*, of course, surpassed) among the brothers here in their daily round. Whenever I wonder about the natural law, the strange logic that co-exists with revealed truth, I think of Maisie – not always, of course, her natural gaiety and wonderment were too often choked by

75

What a curious story Tata told me. This couple (French apparently and very well born) took drugs (it was one of the tragedies of those times). A friend of theirs (a princess! French princesses, of course . . .) shared their tastes, but preferred cocaine to opium (such differences seem somehow only to make it all more degrading!) and one day found what she thought to be cocaine in a small china pot. It was only after she had been taking it for some weeks, that she learned from the maid that she was stealing the ashes of her hostess's father! What a comment on the times!

the stupid greeds and snobberies of her upbringing, and alas! by our too 'sophisticated' failure to understand her – but in her general and underlying mood, her vitality, her animal spirits, her infinite capacity for what we *all* worshipped in the 'twenties but only a few like her understood – 'fun'. She had, of course, the animal's sudden cruelties and the animal's desire to survive at any cost. But no human, of course, *is* an animal, and I have been amazed in these last years (we corresponded weekly) to see how resignation and acceptance were coming upon her without in any *degree* lessening her enjoyment

Tata sent me this picture of the Boulevard Montparnasse in 1925. It shows his friends Mary Butts and Evan Morgan (later an important lord) and Aleister Crowley (a terrible man!).

of life or her amazing vitality. I know what you or Bridget would say – no good works, no social burden – we speak, I fear, across four hundred years' gulf. Like Maisie, I never had the Protestant conscience, like Father, Bridget always had. A life of bridge and library books and old colonels and matinées is not what I would seek. But let us remember, however 'trivial' as you say her days may seem to have become, she too did not choose them. Poor darling! She used to say she would 'give her soul for mink and diamonds and a Delage', thank God! she was never put to the test (although, there are few

temptations of whose failure I would be more sure). In one
sense she 'hated' bridge and South Kensington, but she was the
rare person who accepted and used life in whatever sphere she
was compelled to live. I wish we could all feel as sure of our
own acceptance of God's scheme.

And so with recognition of the four hundred years' chasm,
dear Aunt Alice, let me say no more about the fuller meaning
of Maisie's death – in any case, my duty here is quite another
one than writing. Let me only try to do justice to Maisie by
telling you of some of the memories that have been with me so
vividly since the first cable came. You must imagine them –
these jumbled memories of a silly but well-meaning vanished
age – against an improbable setting of vast snow-capped
mountains, fantastic baroque gateways, tropical vegetation
(reminding me so often of the more vulgar Embassy receptions

of my youth) and a never quite absent sound of surf waves. Viewed so, they have, I hope, something of Firbank, of *Sorrow in Sunlight* about them.

First, Maisie at Rumpelmayer's. It was all that an American, who for all her 'twentyishness' was really an Edwardian, could dream of. Nothing of Saki's duchess, you know, not a lover of *petits fours*, but a real greedy young girl devouring *marron* boats and *meringues chantilly* like a young boa constrictor. She was still, you see, a sort of Daisy Miller long after the corruption about which Henry James made such an absurd fuss had com-

Ronald Firbank, whose novels I have never read, but who was a great friend of Tata's. My great-nephew Timothy says this is VERY *important. A fantastic Spanish marchesa!*

pletely engulfed her. Did ever man understand *real* innocence less?

Maisie sitting on the sofa, surrounded by long-legged pierrots and sausage-shaped cushions, by her side amber holders and black and gold Russian cigarettes, by her other side a box of *marrons glacés*. The room filled with bowls of flowers — sweet peas and crimson rambler roses, can you imagine a more hideous combination? Many of the bowls with real flower heads floating in them among wax water lilies! — anyone else would have been asleep with the tobacco smoke and central heating,

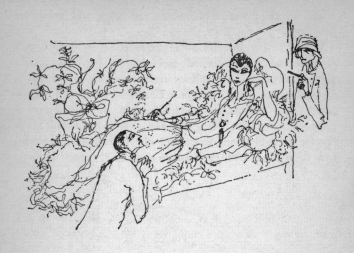

MADONNA OF THE SLEEPING CARS
GENTLEMEN PREFER BLONDES

THE GREEN HAT
LADY CHATTERLEY'S LOVER

the sweet peas and joss sticks! but Maisie, after a heavy dinner, dressed in bead fringing, sat, as intent as a child, over the latest best-seller. Her taste in novels was pure romance! She could never – to her credit – take the solid family realism of Galsworthy or Bennett. She liked romance and she liked shocking books! She was, too, although she was more truly unshockable in real life than her 'shocking' contemporaries, genuinely shocked by 'outspokenness' in print. *The Madonna of the Sleeping Cars* was her favourite book, though *Sweet Pepper* and *Whipped Cream* ran it close. She adored, too, *The Green Hat* and

I was always so happy when I found a picture of my friends in the 'Tatler'. Here they were in Venice in 1928. Tata is already under the influence of the R.C.s. Sybil is with her friend the Princesse de Polignac.

Mayfair. *The Constant Nymph* she thought just silly. She never saw the point of bohemianism without a rich income to back it up – and quite right too. She tried so hard, I remember, with *Gentlemen Prefer Blondes*. But humour and satire were never her strong suit. If people were being witty, she would sit bolt upright, her cigarette holder held a little before her face to disguise her shyness, and, when she thought that something humorous had been said, she would burst out into a polite but entirely artificial laugh. Bridget and I used to be terribly embarrassed by this – in our own different ways, we were

brimming over with sense of humour – but I realize now that Maisie didn't need the self-protection from life that humour provides. When she laughed – and she laughed a great deal – the noise came as a deep and long response to the pleasure of living. She didn't find things 'funny', but she always found life 'fun'. I think one of the most moving pictures I have of her is of the agony she went through trying to read *Lady Chatterley's Lover*. It was, I am glad to say, one of the few occasions on which I saw her trying to perform a duty. 'Poor dears!' she said to me, 'it was so hard for them to have any fun with all that talking about it going on,' and then she added, 'I wish this man hadn't given her a cripple for a husband, it doesn't make very pretty reading.' You see, Aunt Alice, she had all that Lawrence was talking about – please don't think I suppose it was enough – without all his Chapel preaching and board school teacher's gentility. But she did love her library book – a nice romantic story with a coating of harmless smut. 'Darling,' I used to say of some of her favourites, 'you know that not one word of it has the remotest claim to truth. It's just kitchen-maid nonsense, sweetie. Admit now.' 'It's a very nice story, Tata dear,' she would reply; 'I thought the Spanish boy the heroine married was very like Luis. I must read Luis the bit where the heroine watches him gambling and realizes he is just a little excited boy.' 'But, darling,' I would cry, 'Luis isn't just an excited little boy.' He had after all just taken £200 and a pair of ruby cufflinks from Maisie. 'No, perhaps not, Tata, but then the Spanish boy in the book didn't have Luis's wonderful legs, so it was easier for him.'

I think, perhaps, that one cannot really write of Maisie. To describe her sort of directness and pleasure loving, even her sort of silliness, inevitably makes her sound affected. Bridget, when she did not dislike her too much, thought her just that – affected and silly. But then for Bridget life was a complicated, disappointing affair, never simple. She writes to me now to say that she is happy in a more simple setting – dogs and heavy

A Wild Western. Maisie loved them!

No, No Nanette *was such a gay, bright show. Everyone was singing 'I want to be Happy' and 1925 was really a very happy year. Joe Coyne and George Grossmith too, so wonderful for their years.*

What a pretty show Rose Marie *was! The Totem chorus will always remain in my memory. Edith Day and Derek Oldham made the whole thing almost a light opera rather than a musical comedy.*

husbands in tweeds and local good works – I hope so much that she is, but even if she is more content, it could never be Maisie's direct happiness, it could only be a contentment which came from her being in control by a complicated system of moral payments. Maisie never wanted to be in control, she just wanted to have her own way. When she didn't get it she screamed and swore – how she could swear and how she enjoyed it! – but she soon found something else she wanted and had that instead.

Of course, she adored the films. The old silent ones, with all the crying and laughing and rolling of eyes. They were, too,

PAVLOVA – *I was lucky enough to get this picture of the great dancer as a simple ordinary woman.*

*Argentina. I found the castanets
so disturbing to the nerves.*

such wonderful stories. She saw herself as all the heroines, of
course, from Theda Bara through both the Gishes and both the
Talmadges to Clara Bow, every one, I think, except our own
dear English Violet Hopson. Not that she played screen roles
in everyday life, she was much too contented for that. She
merely reacted to 'love' as soon as she saw it, especially if she
knew that there was a good straightforward sexual motive to it.
She had all the flirtatious feeling of her Edwardian childhood,
but without the physical kidgloves, the 'don't touch me now,

Films of the Time

THE CABINET OF DR CALIGARI
THE BLACK PIRATE

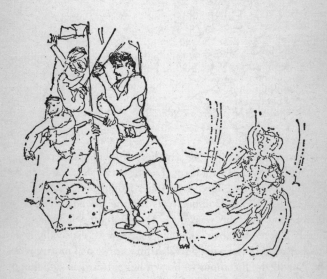

LITTLE LORD FAUNTLEROY
CITY LIGHTS

Maisie at a Spanish cabaret. Her simple American soul easily fancied she could play Carmen.

Harry, please' line which made so many of her equally flirtatious, equally amorous contemporaries so unhappy. If life, in fact, was fun for her, it was never a self-conscious game. I feel sure, perhaps I even hope, that my letter may shock you and Bridget, Aunt Alice, but you asked me to write seriously and I have taken you at your word. In truth, I am just self-indulgent, for I have been so puzzled in thinking about Maisie to discover why so wandering, so lost a soul should seem to me so essentially more saved than a hundred others who have spent their lives in wriggling in and out of conscience's twinges.

How she adored Rudolf Valentino! All her men were cads. Dago dancers, I think Uncle Harold once called them, or the sort of bounderish majors that were only different in not being dago. I found them all *charming*, if a bit boring. Maisie was far too busy adoring and quarrelling ever to be bored. Complicated and self-deceiving bounders or men without the most excessive manners she couldn't abide. Here perhaps she was very un-American, for she liked her men dressed to kill and talking right through her own non-stop chatter. Strong silent men, so popular among the middle classes of her time, she

found just embarrassing. If the strong silence of Tom Mix or William S. Hart had not been disguised by the fact that the films were silent anyway she would never have been such a lover of cowboys. She liked her sheikhs to dance the tango perfectly and the way of an eagle for her lay through the padded carpets and massed hydrangeas of the Ritz or the Crillon. Madame Fahmy, the thunderstorm and the Savoy Hotel always remained her favourite *cause célèbre*, and *causes célèbres* were always her favourite reading.

Mary Pickford she always disliked. Perhaps that little waif recalled her own childhood too clearly, and for Maisie the years before eighteen were always a sheer waste of time. As to the comic genius of Charlie Chaplin, it simply passed her by or

This is the 'baroque' picture by Cocteau which dear Tata says shocked Maisie so much. Evidently something very clever.

worried her as one of those things at which one was supposed to laugh. As for what is now regarded as so essential a part of the 'twenties, decadent or morbid art, she just didn't notice it. If decadent plays or pictures were fashionable she went to see them and thought them 'really very clever', but she always hoped it would be Charlot or Cochran or *No No Nanette* to which she would be taken. I remember once that a clever friend of Sybil Clamber insisted on taking us to see *The Cabinet of Dr Caligari*. Bridget and I screamed ourselves hoarse with terror, and Maisie just went to sleep! She said afterwards that she thought perhaps waxworks were not her favourite things, and that anyway it seemed foolish to take pictures of them.

What she really enjoyed, of course, was the Ballet Russe, but only, I think, because of the colours and the movement and because the people looked beautiful. *L'Après-midi* embarrassed her rather, and *Lac des Cygnes* was a little too slow. She liked pageant and costume so that *Fire Bird* or *Petrouchka* were always her favourites, but then so were the Chauve-Souris. One thing separated her completely from all our bright young friends. She never liked people to laugh at things that were meant to be serious. On the occasion when we went with Sybil Clamber to see Isadora Duncan dance at the Acropolis I laughed myself silly. Maisie was really quite angry with me. The seats, she said, had cost Sybil a lot of money (she always mentioned things like that where people had less than £8,000 a year, because she regarded them as fighting a terrible battle against poverty) and it was not poor Sybil's fault if Isadora Duncan, like all great artists, wasn't always at the height of her form. She just hadn't noticed that the whole thing was so macabre that one had either to laugh or cry with pity. As for that bit of nonsense Jean Cocteau did of me at the time of my conversion – I've had so much baroque since I came to South America that I no longer find it 'amusing' – Maisie thought it was most shocking and begged me *never* to show it to Monsignor, who of course adored it.

A Berlin Night Club in 1924. One sees only too clearly why Hitler came to power! Harold was disgusted – as he said, the French at least know how to make vice elegant.

What, of course, fitted Maisie so nicely into the 'twenties was her childish love of parties and excitement – not as James Douglas used to say 'feverish excitement', but just parties and new faces and new things to do. She adored dressing up – but that was really Edwardian, though she never had the Edwardian love of practical jokes. She took everyone as they came, however peculiar. Some of my own friends, for example, like Eugen. She was perfectly aware of Eugen's behaviour – in sex she was never prudish and naïve – but she wasn't really very interested because it didn't concern her. That was why she was so little nuisance when, to my fury, we visited Berlin *en famille*. As to Eugen's travesties, well, she liked dressing up too, only not in quite such ugly costumes. She had, I now believe, a strange sense of the fragile, passing nature of the happiness to which she clung. She knew that the deep misery into which she could easily be plunged – the 'blues' she would have called it – was not really to be evaded so easily, but she couldn't – poor soul! – find any way of fitting them into her high school, soda-fountain scheme of life. But it did make her good and easy with the washed-up and the defeated like Eugen – she only had one answer it is true – 'Give them what they want' – and it wasn't, of course, adequate, but it helped. Eugen was once or twice quite nice during that visit, only what Maisie couldn't guess at and I knew only too well was that Eugen nice was less a reality than Eugen disgusting. That, of course, is where the 'jes' naturally loving' line of Maisie's beloved Harlem doesn't work, but that seems unimportant. Goodbye, dear aunt, and if you have any sense, take my advice and burn my little note; if Bridget sees it, she'll only kick one of those golden setters that I hear she breeds to such perfection.

Dear Alice,

I have not the taste for the macabre which alone could have allowed me to appreciate your account of Maisie's funeral. No doubt as a family occasion it was no more and no less distressing than such ceremonies usually are. I can only commend Bridget for her unforeseen consideration for *personal* feelings in not expecting or inviting friends and acquaintances.

My considerable regard for Maisie – and it is my intention in this letter to astonish you all a little by telling you of how considerable it was – did not easily accept her personality when it was wedded to genteel or raffish (the difference seems immaterial to me) poverty, still less do I care to connect it with death. Any person worthy of consideration – and Maisie had, unlike most of us, some claim to be considered as a person – must of course meet with oblivion, but it is not a meaningful or interesting meeting. Those who have regarded them in their life should as far as possible ignore it.

When, dear Alice, and it gives me great pleasure at last to be able to say it, my car broke down in an isolated Breton village in 1925, and, as a result of your husband's proffered assistance, our acquaintance was renewed, I was appalled, almost morbidly fascinated to find you quite unchanged from the inchoate, uncertain, easily wounded girl whose 'crush' upon me had blighted my schooldays. You had not then been, you were not at the renewal of our acquaintance, you are not now (so far as I may judge from your letter) a person.

In that very first week in which we were forced into each other's company in Brittany and in those few days in Paris before I was able to make my excuses, you failed to understand – and what was worse attempted to hide that failure – everything that I said. My masquerade as Dante, a blend of private joke and personal conviction far beyond you, led you to place

Our meeting in Brittany, in my stupid way I thought it a happy one. Sybil's letter leaves me under no such illusion!

volumes of the Divina Commedia in crushed morocco by my bedside. You treated Max's superb caricature of me with a terrible sniggering broadmindedness. That the shades of intimacy, the shades even of sex might not be so crudely marked off as your ingenuous eye believed them, never entered your head. A Renaissance relationship, the values of an Orlando were beyond your comprehension. You made, I recall, a fitting member of the audience at the André Maurois *séance* at which I was forced to preside; you made, on the

*Sybil dressed as Dante! A little
private joke which my poor head
apparently failed to comprehend!*

other hand, a most unfitting interruption to my luncheon with
Cocteau. Above all you ruined my evening at the Rue de
Lappe when that most divine of artists sang.

During all this time you talked in alternate envious depreca-
tion and boastful awe of your wealthy American sister-in-law.
You painted to me in exhaustive colours the brilliance of your
nephew, the charm of your niece. More than a thousand times
you described yourself as their 'second mother' in what became a most deadening series of Arabian Nights Entertain-
ments. I was not disappointed in either Tata or Bridget. He
was, as I expected, superficial, hoping by the defects of Nature
and the use of fashionable catch-phrases to be thought a second
Ronald Firbank. Firbank, of course, was a person, your
nephew was not. His adoption of the fashionable Roman
Catholic superstitions in the early 'thirties did not, as he may
have hoped, disprove this difference. Bridget was a vapid
débutante, in whom students of the morbid might have found
some interest by the addition of a certain vicious malice towards her mother. It was not, I think, so much – merely a
peevishness due to the recognition of her own inferiority. Her
adoption of the role of county wife and mother I find no more
important than Tata's conversion. Maisie, alone, proved more

The picture Sybil makes such a fuss about in her letter to me. It has something to do with Rossetti, but except that Sybil couldn't leave Lytton Strachey alone I don't really quite follow it. As Harold says, there will always be a set that must be cleverer than their neighbours!

than I expected. I have often told myself that I overestimated her because of the foolish denigrations I had just heard, but with all her limitations – she was totally uneducated in eye, ear and brain – she had nevertheless a certain instinct for immediate living, a highly developed intuitive sense of atmosphere which allowed her to be noticed by persons of talent, even genius, whose lives were dedicated to communication and expression on a personal level. I saw a good deal of her until the failure of her fortune. I have no doubt that she preserved more than most of us in that disaster. But adversity and poverty

cannot enrich anyone and I do not in consequence seek the company of those who suffer from them. In all those years, I suggested to her again and again that I had no wish to see the rest of her family; but it was part of her natural Middle Western

Paris, 1926.
Damia sings in the Rue de Lappe.

personality that she begged me not to 'hurt others', particularly you who had introduced us. In others I would have thought such arguments sentimentalism, but in Maisie they were an integral generosity of spirit which I had no desire to emulate but had naturally to respect. In the literary world in which I moved she was always accepted. The extracts from various works which I enclose will show you that she even impinged. It is interesting to note that she had some effect upon the writer of the short story who, of course, was dead before I knew her.

I suppose that I should explain my letter by saying conventionally that we are both old women now and can no longer be hurt, but, after reading again *your* letter about Maisie, I am unable to wish for so innocuous an ending to our 'friendship'.

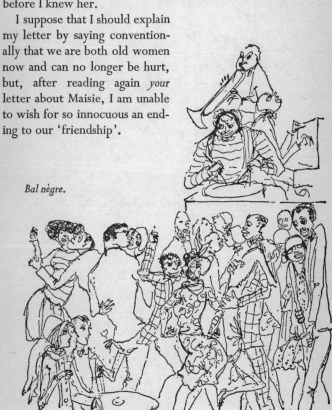

Bal nègre.

These are snaps I took of Sybil at the parties she mentions in her letters. The meeting of André Maurois (he was so brilliant, I could have listened all day) and the meeting with Cocteau, which I apparently so unhappily spoilt!

Maisie's odd moments in literature

(Katherine Mansfield)

1. In an unpublished short story of which it has been said that 'though the author put it aside, did not indeed even include it among the fragments of her journal, it has nevertheless something about it so completely natural, so entirely momentary and real that one wonders once again at the arbitrary manner of critics who assert "Here life ends, here art begins"'. The story (or more truly vignette) tells of a young girl's shopping expedition from Bayswater (the atmosphere of which the author characteristically catches as 'The North Side of the Park') to Bond Street. The tone of the little sketch may be caught from the tentative title given it by the author *Shopping Beyond our Means*, though in the margin she had written 'S. behind the Scenes?' and again 'S. Beyond our Teens?' 'The chinchilla woman' (Maisie, in fact), she writes, 'I actually saw one day outside Asprey's, but she reminded me so irresistibly by something about the mouth of Sophie G-B. that I was taken back to all those old quarrels and the impossibilities of it . . .' The paragraph at the end (?) of the little sketch which embodies 'the chinchilla woman' (Maisie) runs as follows – 'Lena stood for a moment on the kerb and watched the great red buses engulfing the rest of the traffic, swallowing up taxicabs and motorcars, refusing no doubt the hawkers' barrows and the passing butcher boy on his bicycle. She gazed at the top of the great scarlet monster, at the forms grey and shapeless in the dull February light, and then, suddenly an orange shape among them. A woman carrying a tropical bird. More likely a bag of oranges. It always was, she decided, a bag of oranges and never a tropical bird. Two men, so well dressed – oh how lovely to be so well dressed despite the dull February day, to decide in the morning that you would put this on and that, not to have to wear the old olive green hat that only made the day seem

more foggy – in each of their mouths a black cigar stump. Like
the beards on mussels, she decided. And then suddenly from
the jewellers, from Aladdin's cave (for it might as well have
been Aladdin's cave for her, Lena decided, when one thought
of the ten shillings so carefully folded by Aunt Penelope before
she handed it over and still reposing unbroken – could one
break a ten shilling note, she wondered – at the bottom of her
old black velvet reticule so threadbare at the seams) there
stepped the chinchilla woman. Stout and handsome and com-
manding, and so happy, Lena felt sure, sleek like a velvety cat.
"Put those in the back of the motor," she called to the
chauffeur. What could "those" be? Lena reflected. Two diamond tiaras, no doubt, or bangles of ruby and sapphire. Oh

happy chinchilla woman to say "those" so easily. And suddenly Lena felt as though she were walking on air, as though the whole of Bond Street were sailing away in the clouds, and the lights in the shop windows that were greeting the closing afternoon seemed stars shimmering, winking . . .'

2. *From the diary of a successful novelist of the period.* (Arnold Bennett)

Talked to one of Northcliffe's secretaries today. He told me that when the Old Man took his trips to the Riviera or the Pyrenees, he had as many as 500 dispatch boxes made ready in Fleet Street in case of need. S.T. who wrote for them in '19 received as much as £300 per 298 words (but ghosts were completely barred!). The still-room maids at Claridges get £3 10s. a week and 'perks'! but the latter have rapidly decreased since the Armistice. Mariette at the Hotel des Ponts et Chausées got 6 francs a week in the old days! Forster says somewhere that Charles Dickens wrote 16,000 words a day at the time when Chapmans were pressing him for the serial parts of *Dombey*. (This needs checking.) Met an American cousin of T.G.'s, Maisie Blade, at Sybil's after dinner. Big handsome woman but talked too much. Struck me as having the right feeling for living though. Her daughter Bridget, a well turned-out girl with very pretty legs, tells me she is doing mannequin work. All these girls nowadays feel they have to 'do' something. Current novel: 2,000 w. Article on 'Inn Signs and English Literature': 2,000 w. Weekly article: 1,500 w.

3. *She appears as a very subsidiary character in the work of a more highbrow popular novelist.* (Aldous Huxley)

'Ah! dear lady,' Professor Raglan fluted. His voice, they said, has risen a semitone or more since the telegram came after the Ypres salient. Rodney dead, the fair young flesh shattered, the Alpha mind, the young hands that steered the bicycle up the

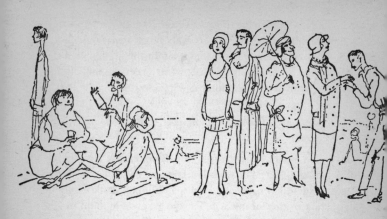

Photograph from the 'Tatler' of Biarritz in 1927.
More than one royal personage present!

Iffley Road destroyed, putrescent now, green beneath those poppy-laden fields. By smiting the first born shall the fathers be emasculated. 'You seek, I fear, for chinoiserie where none exists. Nothing of that elegant age here. Absint Beaumarchais and Diderot. *Imprimé à* Pekin. How charmingly the liberal and the deistic *clientes* sought to evade autocracy's censorship! Nor is it the deep calm, the peony-laden wisdom of true Pekin, of,' his fluting faltered, 'of Confucius,' he ended lamely. The Humanities did not, he reflected dryly, include a training in Oriental philosophies. 'No, no, dear lady, the Pekin Man died alone and curiously. That bitten arm, I often reflect upon it. A race of autophagi. But where did they begin on their slow, their painfully slow self-destruction? Succulently, fatly like good little pygophiles at the buttocks; a difficult operation, nor would the coccyx prove very delicious; or boldly, more

decidedly at the very citadel of fruition. A difficult decision. Not that our *ancêtre pékinois* stood alone. St Coprophilus, for example, on emerging from the Ravenna Marshes. He flourished, you know, at the very moment of that most tedious sophist Boethius. Though he was not, I imagine,' and he laughed a piccolo note, 'one of that gentleman's "consolations" for slow compression of the arteries. St Coprophilus ate the whole of his own right leg, though as it was already mortifying we may suppose him to have liked his meat high. He too, perished, though. Those that live by the flesh, you know.' He gazed at the sleek, black-satined figure of his hostess. There seemed little prospect of Arachne Sweetall (Maisie) perishing. She thrived, it seemed, on self-generated *joie de vivre*. Golden lads, perhaps, and chimney sweepers, but not, it appeared, hostesses. He turned away in disgust.

Sybil adored Isadora Duncan! Here she is dancing at the Acropolis (see Tata's letter).

4. She 'occurs' in a novel of an eminent woman writer of the time. (Virginia Woolf)

'And now Lord and Lady Chalmers. Who could that be? Charles, of course, how silly of her. Charles and Myra. Charles so distinguished and tired, and Myra intense and preoccupied as under the elm trees at Hadlow twenty years ago, but a little breathless now. They had, of course, a whole Viceroyalty behind them, so that if they seemed tired . . . Carrie thought. As they came towards her up the stairs, she sensed processions, and elephants with great painted howdahs, and strange Hindu gods violent in colour, gimcrack. She would have liked to have visited India, indeed had been going in 1912 with Aunt Rachel, when Michael had appeared and, of course . . . There were so many here tonight that she did not know – that thin Frenchman just too inclined to be *really* attentive and that large dark American woman (Maisie) with a curious, coarse happiness. She turned away offended at the unwanted freshness of it. Hibbert, at least, she knew. Hibbert handing round the champagne. Hibbert who had been with them so long that she even knew of his crippled mother in Buckinghamshire, had indeed once sent Dr Graves there when she was ill with pneumonia. And at the thought of Hibbert's crippled mother, she was suddenly once more in the flower shop of this morning, the delay and the woman's anxious face, "Yes, milady, 17 Green Street. Forgive us, milady, our son died this morning. Meningitis. He had just taken a scholarship." It was absurd of Helen to have worn that white dress at her age. She turned away frowning. And then suddenly she knew the party was a success. She could almost hear them crying it, "Carrie's done it again." "Carrie's occasions never fail." She looked across at where Michael was talking so solemnly to that Dutch diplomat, of all things, of bottled beer. Catching her eye, he smiled back at her, thanking her for it all, the success and the occasion. Smiling, she thought of how little he knew of the effort that had preceded it.'

113

Nissia Sert, Diaghilev, Stravinsky, Picasso.

A Bloomsbury group! Sybil was always at home here!

A Bohemian party. All brilliant people, I believe, but looking at the snap, it might be Barnum and Bailey's.

Letter from Captain Toby Buller to
Maisie's grandson Timothy

Dear old Tim,

I ought to be angry at a young fellow of your age offering money to a man who is old enough to be your grandfather, but I can't be. Now that your grandmother's gone, I don't suppose I shall be long in following her to that bourne whence no traveller returns as old Bill Shakespeare puts it. I've had a good life, and though I've certainly been no plaster cast saint, I don't suppose that when they shout the odds at the end (or whatever arrangements they make up there) I shall necessarily be barred from the field. You ask me to say quite honestly how I am placed financially, and quite honestly I must answer you that I'm nowhere near in the first three, in fact financially I'm a non-starter. The little pension that the Government saw fit to give us for doing what we had to against Kaiser William just doesn't make sense in these days of the 'welfare state', and, though I flatter myself that with a normal run of luck at cards I could just about double it, any gambler who's not a fool knows he must have a spot of capital behind him.

When you say that it would have made your grandmother happy to have known that I would have the money she left you, I think you're on to more than you know. Bless her old Edwardian heart! dear boy, for all her easygoing ways, she liked to preserve the social conventions. I don't think I could have loved her as I did, if she hadn't. Of course, she would have liked you to have had the money, we both would have done. You don't realize perhaps that I like to think your visits to the hotel here were a bit for both the old codgers. I wish to God she'd had enough to leave to both of us, but even if she had, she wouldn't have put me in her will. Not for your mother and your great-aunt, with all due respect to them, to have had the chance to cry stinking fish. So far as the little

The last snap of Maisie at the Haigheath Hotel. With that terrible Toby Buller!

income goes, I accept it, and I respect you for understanding her real wishes. As to the rest of the stuff, the bits of furniture, scrap books and so on, you must come and collect them whenever you wish. Youth's a strangely sentimental age, and should be. Or shall I say that sentiment goes rather deeper than that when you get to my age? God bless you! dear boy.

Extracts from Maisie's diary

1920. MY! what a day! Shopping with Alice is the limit. I don't know which she enjoys more, refusing gifts she'd like to have or noting things she'd like which I didn't offer to buy for her. I tried both all the afternoon, and packed her off to Weybridge in the car happy as a schoolgirl because she made me feel the new platinum speaking tube was common and because she could call at Lady Archer's on the way and show it off to her. English pleasures, oh dear! oh golly! What I hate is that she keeps making me think Gerald was that way really. But he wasn't! and anyway he was *so* goodlooking! Oh! I do miss his looks. Bridget makes me cry she's so like him to look at, even when she's wishing I was more like dear Aunt Alice. Now I shall have a long, long hot bath with gardenia bath salts and lots of candy. And then I shall dance and dance Alice out of my poor head. If he's like he was Thursday, he'll be wonderful.

1925. I can't let Bridget play around with the poor lamb a day longer. She's no right to get her pleasure that way, leading him on and then 'But, Mummy darling, I didn't for a moment imagine he was serious. After all because he dances so divinely that he's a professional doesn't really mean that one wants . . .' I hate women! I'm just going to wade right in and win. Besides he *does* dance divinely and he has the cutest nose. And I'm getting old. And so what?

1927. Tata's so pretty I don't like him being in a rage. But Dick Mutton's too nice for all that nonsense. For it *is* nonsense. Not for Eugen and all the funnies, but for Dick it is. Oh! how I love him. And I'm old enough to be his mother. And we laugh and laugh when we're together! And it won't last. And I don't care. I shall give Tata a wonderful trip round the world. He mustn't be unhappy. He doesn't get his fun that way like Bridget, and he shan't have to!

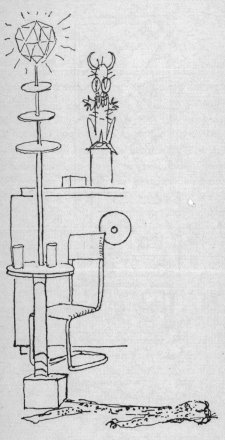

1928. Sybil and all her friends! Oh, what a lot of talk! Some of it so good when I can follow and some just so plain dumb. I wish she wasn't so mean. She's not mean like Alice or Bridget who don't know it, she just feels mean about people and sees no reason to change it. My! what an uncomfortable way to live. Better than Aunt Mary's though, except the old thing does have fun in her way with her speeches and her aeroplanes. Telling the poor where to put it! I don't know why she

Fancy Dress
Tata as Tutankhamen's Widow

Bridget as
'Bubbles'

Myself in
Venetian gown

doesn't get scragged. I guess the worst thing about being poor is that it makes you too low even to scrag busybodies like Aunt Mary. Well! Juan-les-Pins tomorrow and everybody just the same as here only with less clothes on. And the funny thing is I don't seem to get one bit tired of it. 'You sleep the sun is shining, you wake the day's declining, you're tired, you're uninspired, you're blasé.' That must be somebody else is all I can say.

Two friends of Maisie's — and strictly between ourselves, rather common! Jeannette Landseer's husband was a war profiteer, she thought of nothing but gambling. Poor Mrs Oldroyd hadn't an 'h' to her name, but quite a good heart really.

1950. Oh dear! how nice Timothy is, and how solemn. And how I adore him! Not the faintest bit like his mother. And so polite to Toby. Poor Toby! he's so awful when people treat him like a gentleman. I used to think he once must have known the answers, but now I'm afraid it just isn't true. But how nice he is and how nice it is to have one's man, even when he pawns everything within reach. I've left the little that's still there to Timothy, but, of course, Toby'll have it off him. But it'll make Timothy happy to give it and people now have so little opportunity of giving. It's the next thing to men and clothes that I've liked most. Oh dear! I don't look forward to Halibut, sauce hollandaise and Pear Condé, but never mind, we're going to the movies afterwards and it's Stewart Granger.

The men in Maisie's *life!*

MORE ABOUT PENGUINS
AND PELICANS

Penguinews, which appears every month, contains details of all the new books issued by Penguins as they are published. From time to time it is supplemented by *Penguins in Print*, which is our complete list of almost 5,000 titles.

A specimen copy of *Penguinews* will be sent to you free on request. Please write to Dept EP, Penguin Books Ltd, Harmondsworth, Middlesex, for your copy.

In the U.S.A.: For a complete list of books available from Penguins in the United States write to Dept CS, Penguin Books, 625 Madison Avenue, New York, New York 10022.

In Canada: For a complete list of books available from Penguins in Canada write to Penguin Books Canada Ltd, 41 Steelcase Road West, Markham, Ontario.